O9-BTO-234

The Fairy Princess

A SPOOKY, SPARKLY HALLOWEEN

by Julie Andrews & Emma Walton Hamilton

Illustrated by
Christine Davenier

Little, Brown and Company
New York Boston

BOO!
It's me, Gerry, the very fairy princess!
You might not recognize me, because I'm wearing
a costume...but I'm still a fairy princess underneath.
(You can take the princess out of her sparkles,
but you can't take the sparkle out of a princess!)

ALLEN COUNTY PUBLIC LIBRARY

I'm trying out costumes because I'm getting ready
for a VERY special day next week.
It's HALLOWEEN!

We get to wear our costumes to school, and we're going to have a big parade with prizes before we go out trick-or-treating. I can't WAIT to see what all my friends will look like!

The problem is, I'm having a hard time choosing a costume that works with my wings and crown.

Daddy says, "Just go as a fairy princess!"
"That's not a COSTUME," I say.
"That's what I AM!"

Mommy says she knows I'll come up with something creative.

My brother, Stewart, says, "How about a drama queen?"
I choose to ignore this.
(Fairy princesses know how
to rise above poor manners.)

I have a THOUSAND ideas…

…but nothing
seems quite right.
What am I going to do?

Suddenly, it comes to me.

I'll be an angel!

I'll drape a sheet over my dress, KEEP my wings and crown,

and just add a sparkly halo.

PERFECT!
(Fairy princesses always come through in a pinch.)

On Halloween morning, Daddy makes pumpkin muffins. YUM!
When he sees my costume, he says, “There’s my little angel!”

I have to admit, Stewart looks pretty cool as a baseball hero.
Mommy straightens my halo.
"You've really out-sparkled yourself!" she says.

At school, a giant bunny greets us at the door.
It's Mr. Bonario!
The classroom looks fun and spooky,
but the BEST part is seeing everyone's costumes.
José is a musketeer, Cody Rose is a pop star, and Patrick is an astronaut.

My best friend, Delilah, is a dentist—
that's what she wants to be when she grows up.
She also wants to remind everyone about "dental hygiene"
after all the Halloween candy.
(Fairy princesses have the most thoughtful friends!)

At lunchtime, Connor, who is dressed as
a zombie sock monkey, sits at our table.
He is pounding ketchup onto his hot dog when suddenly
it SQUIRTS all over Delilah's dentist jacket.
"NOW it looks more like a Halloween costume!" he jokes.

But it's NOT funny.
"I can't wear this
in the parade!"
Delilah cries.
"It sends TOTALLY
the wrong message
about dentists!"

Time for a fairy princess to work some magic!

I look around the classroom.

Then I look at my own costume. LIGHTBULB!

“You can still remind everyone about dental hygiene,” I say.

“Watch this!”

I take off my sheet and turn it upside down.
"Step in!" I tell Delilah.

Then I stuff paper towels all around her, staple the edges of the sheet, and tie knots at her shoulders.

I stand back to look at my work.
"See?" I say. "Now you're a TOOTH!"

Delilah blinks away her tears. “But what about YOUR costume?” she asks.

“It’s okay,” I say. “I have my wings and crown.

Some people think that’s a costume anyway.”

(Fairy princesses have to make sacrifices for friends in need.)

“Wait!” Delilah says. “If I’m a tooth, why can’t YOU be my tooth fairy?”

BRILLIANT!

We grab construction paper, scissors, glitter, and glue.

We have to work fast.

The parade is about to begin!

All the classes are already lining up outside.
Scary organ music is coming through the loudspeaker,
and our music teacher, Mr. Higginbottom, is banging a drum.

Parents and teachers are standing
on the path, taking pictures.
We join the end of the line just in time!

Hand in hand, Delilah and I march with
our WHOLE school to the playground.
We sparkle from the tips of our teeth to the tops of our toes!

We line up on the bleachers, and Mr. Bonario picks up a microphone. "I've been asked to give out the prizes today," he says. "EVERYONE here is a winner—but I think we can all agree that an award for creative teamwork must go to...Gerry and Delilah!"

The audience cheers. Mom and Dad look amazed.
Stewart gives us two thumbs up.
Even Connor does a happy dance!

Mr. Bonario hands us a BIG box of chocolates, and winks.
"Just remember to brush afterward!" he says.

As we take our bows, Delilah squeezes my hand.

"You may be a fairy princess," she whispers,
"but today you were an angel in disguise!"

For the village of Sag Harbor—
nobody does Halloween better!

—J.A. & E.W.H.

For Douglas and John with all my love.

—C.D.

About This Book

The illustrations for this book were done in ink and color pencil on Kaecolor paper.

The text was set in Baskerville and the display type is Mayfair.

This book was edited by Liza Baker and designed by Phil Caminiti with art direction by Patti Ann Harris.

The production was supervised by Erika Schwartz, and the production editor was Christine Ma.

Text copyright © 2015 by Julie Andrews Trust—1989 and Beech Tree Books, LLC • Illustrations copyright © 2015 by Christine Davenier • Cover art © 2015 by Christine Davenier • Cover design by Patti Ann Harris and Phil Caminiti • Cover © 2015 Hachette Book Group, Inc. • All rights reserved. In accordance with the U.S. Copyright Act of 1976, the scanning, uploading, and electronic sharing of any part of this book without the permission of the publisher is unlawful piracy and theft of the author's intellectual property. If you would like to use material from the book (other than for review purposes), prior written permission must be obtained by contacting the publisher at permissions@hbgusa.com. Thank you for your support of the author's rights. • Little, Brown and Company • Hachette Book Group • 1290 Avenue of the Americas, New York, NY 10019 • Visit our website at lb-kids.com • Little, Brown and Company is a division of Hachette Book Group, Inc. • The Little, Brown name and logo are trademarks of Hachette Book Group, Inc. • The publisher is not responsible for websites (or their content) that are not owned by the publisher. • First Edition: August 2015 • Library of Congress Cataloging-in-Publication Data • Andrews, Julie. • The very fairy princess : a spooky, sparkly Halloween / by Julie Andrews & Emma Walton Hamilton ; illustrated by Christine Davenier.—First edition. • pages cm • Summary: "Gerry comes up with a creative Halloween costume, but when her best friend, Delilah, has a costume emergency, the very fairy princess makes a sacrifice that lets her sparkle"—Provided by publisher. • ISBN 978-0-316-28304-5 (hardcover) • [1. Costume—Fiction. 2. Halloween—Fiction. 3. Friendship—Fiction. 4. Schools—Fiction. 5. Princesses—Fiction.] I. Hamilton, Emma Walton. II. Davenier, Christine, illustrator. III. Title. • PZ7.A5673Vee 2015 • [E]—dc23 • 2013046303 • 10 9 8 7 6 5 4 3 2 1 • SC • Printed in China